D0238932

First published in 2007 by
Franklin Watts
338 Euston Road
London
NW1 3BH

Franklin Watts Australia
Level 17/207 Kent Street
Sydney
NSW 2000

A CIP catalogue record for this book is available
from the British Library.

ISBN 978 0 7496 7075 7 (hbk)
ISBN 978 0 7496 7419 9 (pbk)

Series Editor: Melanie Palmer
Series Advisor: Dr Barrie Wade
Series Designer: Peter Scoulding

Printed in China

Franklin Watts is a division of Hachette Children's Books.

The
Pied Piper
of Hamelin

by Penny Dolan and Martin Impey

W
FRANKLIN WATTS
LONDON•SYDNEY

Once there was a rich town
where the people had plenty
of everything.

There were certainly plenty of rats
in the town! They stole food from
the dishes.

They made nests in every bed
and cupboard.

They fought the dogs …

… and chased the cats!

The rats even bit the babies!

"You must get rid of the rats!"

the people told the Mayor.

So the Mayor put up a poster and offered a reward to remove the rats. The people waited and waited.

One day, a tall man appeared. He was dressed in strange clothes of different colours.

"I am the Pied Piper and I can get rid of your rats. But you must pay me a thousand gold coins," he said.

The Mayor whispered something to his deputy. Then he spoke loudly: "Piper, of course we will pay you your reward."

As the Pied Piper stepped into the street, he began to play a magic tune. All the rats stopped and listened.

The rats came running after the
Pied Piper. They ran faster and
faster.

The Piper stopped at the river,
but his music did not. Nor did
the rats.

They ran straight into the
rushing river, and that was
the end of them!

When the Pied Piper went to ask
for his reward, the Mayor laughed.
"You fool! The rats are gone now.
Take these few coins, and get out!"

The Piper was very angry.

"You will be sorry you broke

your promise to me," he said.

The Piper went out into the street.
He lifted his pipe to his lips,
and blew. At once, all the
children ran from the houses.

The children sang and danced, and laughed. They followed the Pied Piper's wonderful tune right out of the town.

Everyone was alarmed.

"Stop him! Pay him!"

they shouted at the Mayor.

"He cannot take them far,"
laughed the Mayor. "Look,
the mountain is in his way."

However, as the Pied Piper reached the mountain, it opened up.

All the children followed the Piper
and his music to a beautiful land.

Then the rocks closed. The children
and the Pied Piper were never seen
again. Only one poor child was
left outside the mountain.

Forever afterwards, the people
of that town were sad and silent.

How the Mayor wished he had
kept his promise!

Hopscotch has been specially designed to fit the requirements of the National Literacy Strategy. It offers real books by top authors and illustrators for children developing their reading skills. There are 43 Hopscotch stories to choose from:

* hardback